Best Friends Forever

Julianne Moore

illustrated by
LeUyen Pham

BLOOMSBURY

NEW YORK BERLIN LONDON SYDNEY

First published in the United States of America in September 2011
by Bloomsbury Books for Young Readers
www.bloomsburykids.com

For information about permission to reproduce selections from this book, write to
Permissions, Bloomsbury BFYR, 175 Fifth Avenue, New York, New York 10010

The painting in this book is based on *Bridge over a Pond of Water Lilies* by Claude Monet. 1899.
Oil on canvas, 36½ x 29 in. (92.7 x 73.7 cm).

Library of Congress Cataloging-in-Publication Data
Moore, Julianne.
Freckleface Strawberry : best friends forever / Julianne Moore ; illustrated by LeUyen Pham.
p.   cm.
Summary: Freckleface Strawberry and Windy Pants Patrick are best friends because they have so much in
common, but when the boys convince Windy Pants that he should play with them at recess, and the girls
convince Freckleface Strawberry to play with them, the friends see that they are very different, too.
ISBN 978-1-59990-551-8 (hardcover) • ISBN 978-1-59990-552-5 (reinforced)
[1. Best friends—Fiction. 2. Friendship—Fiction. 3. Sex role—Fiction. 4. Freckles—Fiction.]
I. Pham, LeUyen, ill. II. Title. III. Title: Best friends forever.
PZ7.M78635 Frf 2011   [E]—dc22   2011013276
ISBN 978-1-59990-782-6 (paperback)

Illustrations rendered with a Japanese brush pen and digitally colored
Typeset in Bodoni Six Book and Minya Nouvelle
Book design by Donna Mark

Printed in China by C&C Offset Printing Co., Ltd., Shenzhen, Guangdong
2 4 6 8 10 9 7 5 3 1 (hardcover)
2 4 6 8 10 9 7 5 3 1 (reinforced)
2 4 6 8 10 9 7 5 3 1 (paperback)

All papers used by Bloomsbury Publishing, Inc., are natural, recyclable products
made from wood grown in well-managed forests. The manufacturing processes
conform to the environmental regulations of the country of origin.

To my sister Valerie, my BFF

—J. M.

To Sweet Alize

—L. P.

Once, Freckleface Strawberry
had a best friend.

They were very much alike.
That's why they were friends.

They were both unusual sizes.

They both had nicknames at school.

They both had families.

They both loved to read.

They both liked lunch, only not in the cafeteria.

They both loved to play.

And they both LOVED trips to the museum.

They stuck up for each other.
They were best friends, forever, all the time.

Until one day . . .

Windy Pants Patrick did not think the boy was right,
but he didn't play with Freckleface Strawberry at recess.

So Freckleface Strawberry watched Windy Pants play ball with the boys. She played jungle-gym monkeys with the rest of the girls.

Boys stink. I don't know why you play with Patrick. You know why they call him Windy Pants, don't you? Besides, he only loves to play ball.

That's not true. He loves to read and eat lunch, and we both have nicknames.

But Freckleface did not wait for
Windy Pants after school that day.

The next day, Windy Pants played with the boys,
and Freckleface played with the girls.

It's not so bad. There are girls who like
lunch and like to read. And besides,
Windy and I are too different.

This is so much better. I don't have to bend down to talk to a short person, and I don't have to play scary monster ever again.

Those other kids are right!

And so they did all the regular stuff that kids do.

Freckleface Strawberry kept going to the museum.

Windy Pants Patrick kept reading books.

And they both kept eating lunch.

But it wasn't the same.

Until one day . . . Freckleface Strawberry was on the playground, looking for a game of ball. She couldn't find any kids, just one big kid playing monster.

Hey, kid! Want to play some ball?

Ball-playing monsters? I would play that all day!
And do you want to have lunch?

And that's when they realized . . .

. . . it didn't matter how different they were because

they were a LOT alike too!

They both liked lunch.
They both liked reading.
They both had hair.
They both had feet.
They both had eyes and skin.
And teeth.

But mostly, they both liked each other.

Which is why they were best friends.
Forever.